I0797420

MOTO X
John Willis
EYEDISCOVER
57

Go to **www.eyediscover.com** and enter this book's unique code.

BOOK CODE

AVA96966

EYEDISCOVER brings you optic readalongs that support active learning.

Published by AV² by Weigl
350 5th Avenue, 59th Floor New York, NY 10118
Website: www.eyediscover.com

Library of Congress Control Number: 2018954182

ISBN 978-1-4896-8037-2 (hardcover)

Printed in the United States of America
in Brainerd, Minnesota
1 2 3 4 5 6 7 8 9 0 22 21 20 19 18

082018
120917

Project Coordinator: John Willis
Designer: Mandy Christiansen

Weigl acknowledges Alamy, Getty Images, Shutterstock, Dreamstime, and iStock as the primary image suppliers for this title.

EYEDISCOVER provides enriched content, optimized for tablet use, that supplements and complements this book. EYEDISCOVER books strive to create inspired learning and engage young minds in a total learning experience.

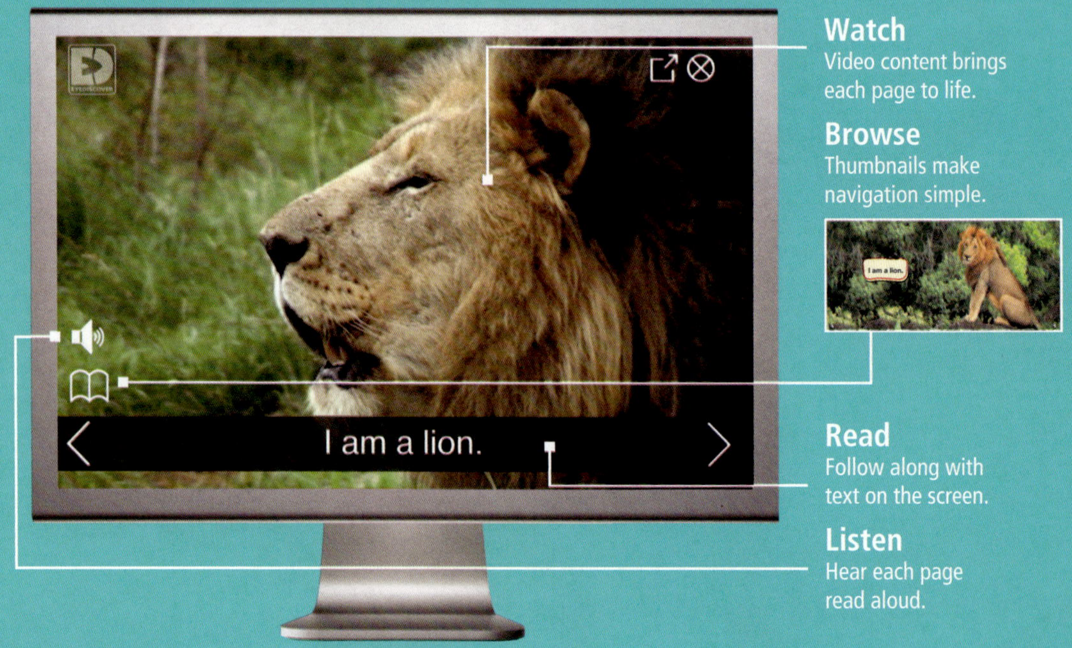

Watch
Video content brings each page to life.

Browse
Thumbnails make navigation simple.

Read
Follow along with text on the screen.

Listen
Hear each page read aloud.

Your EYEDISCOVER Optic Readalongs come alive with...

Audio
Listen to the entire book read aloud.

Video
High resolution videos turn each spread into an optic readalong.

OPTIMIZED FOR

- TABLETS
- WHITEBOARDS
- COMPUTERS
- AND MUCH MORE!

In this book, you will learn about

- what it is
- where it is done
- how it is done

and much more!

Moto X is an extreme sport. Riders use motorcycles to race and jump on offroad tracks.

Moto X bikes are specially built. They are small and sturdy.

TTR
YAMAHA

93

These bikes do not weigh very much. This helps riders jump more easily.

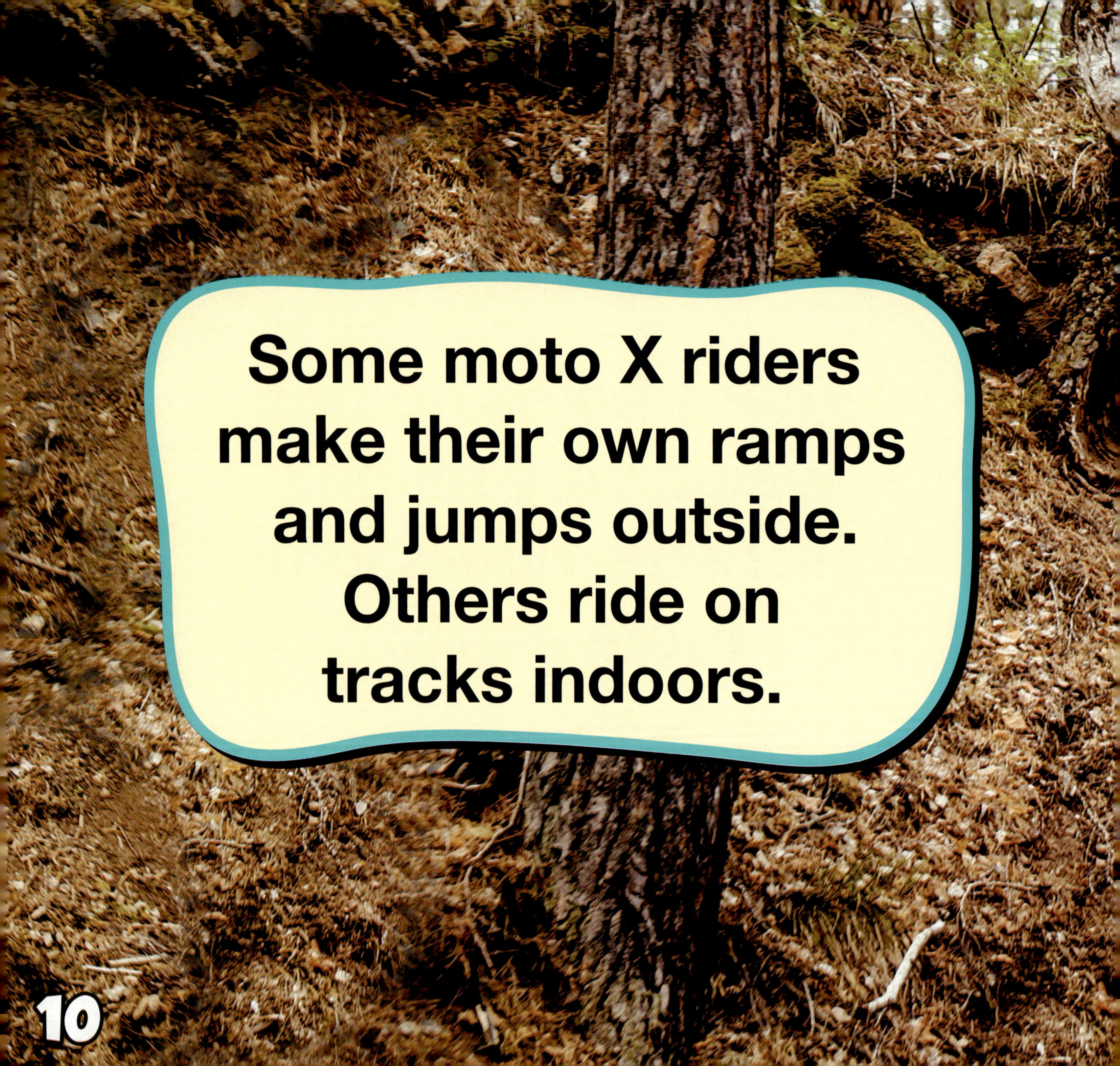

Some moto X riders make their own ramps and jumps outside. Others ride on tracks indoors.

Professional moto X riders practice every day. This helps them compete in different events.

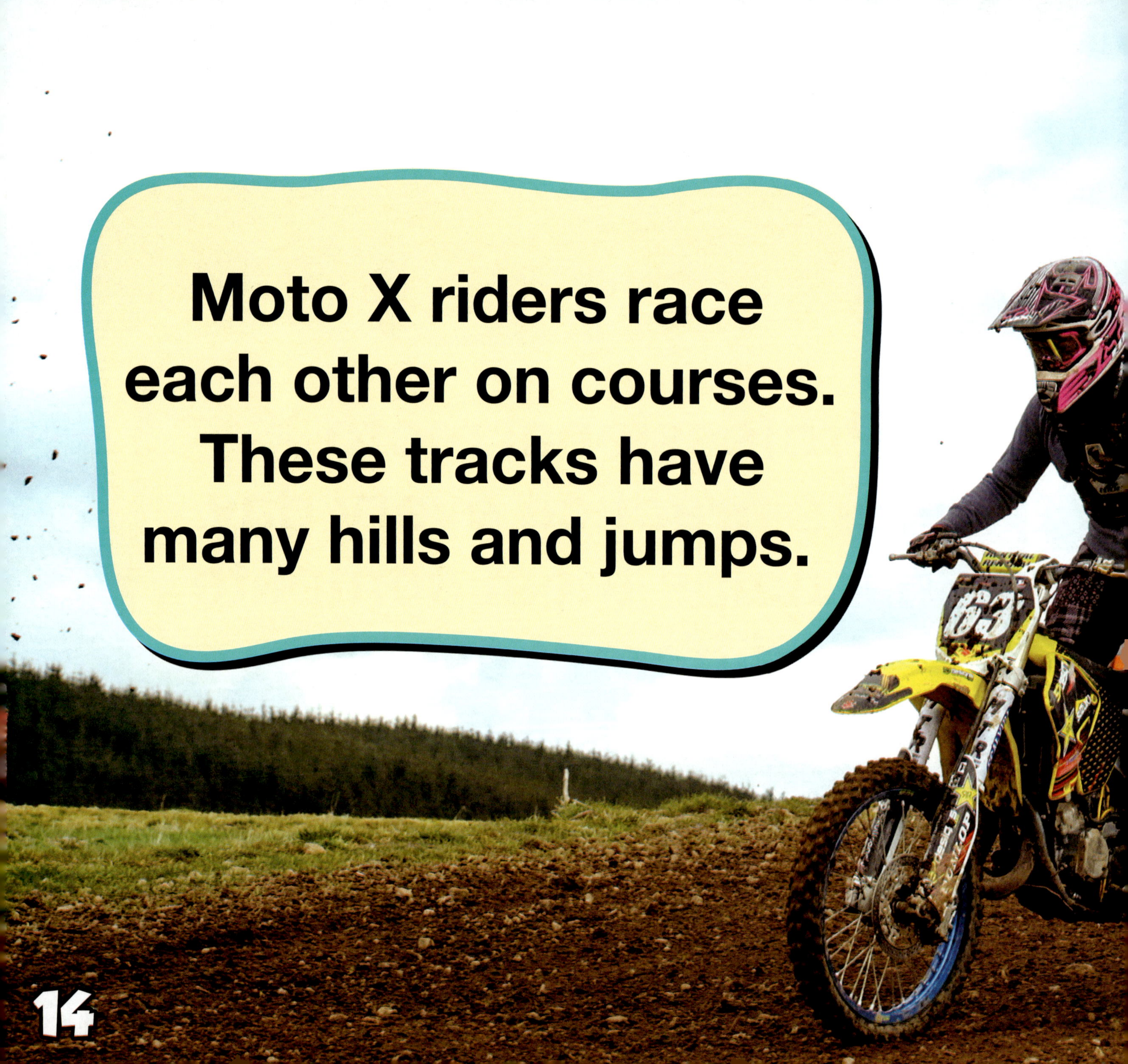

Moto X riders race each other on courses. These tracks have many hills and jumps.

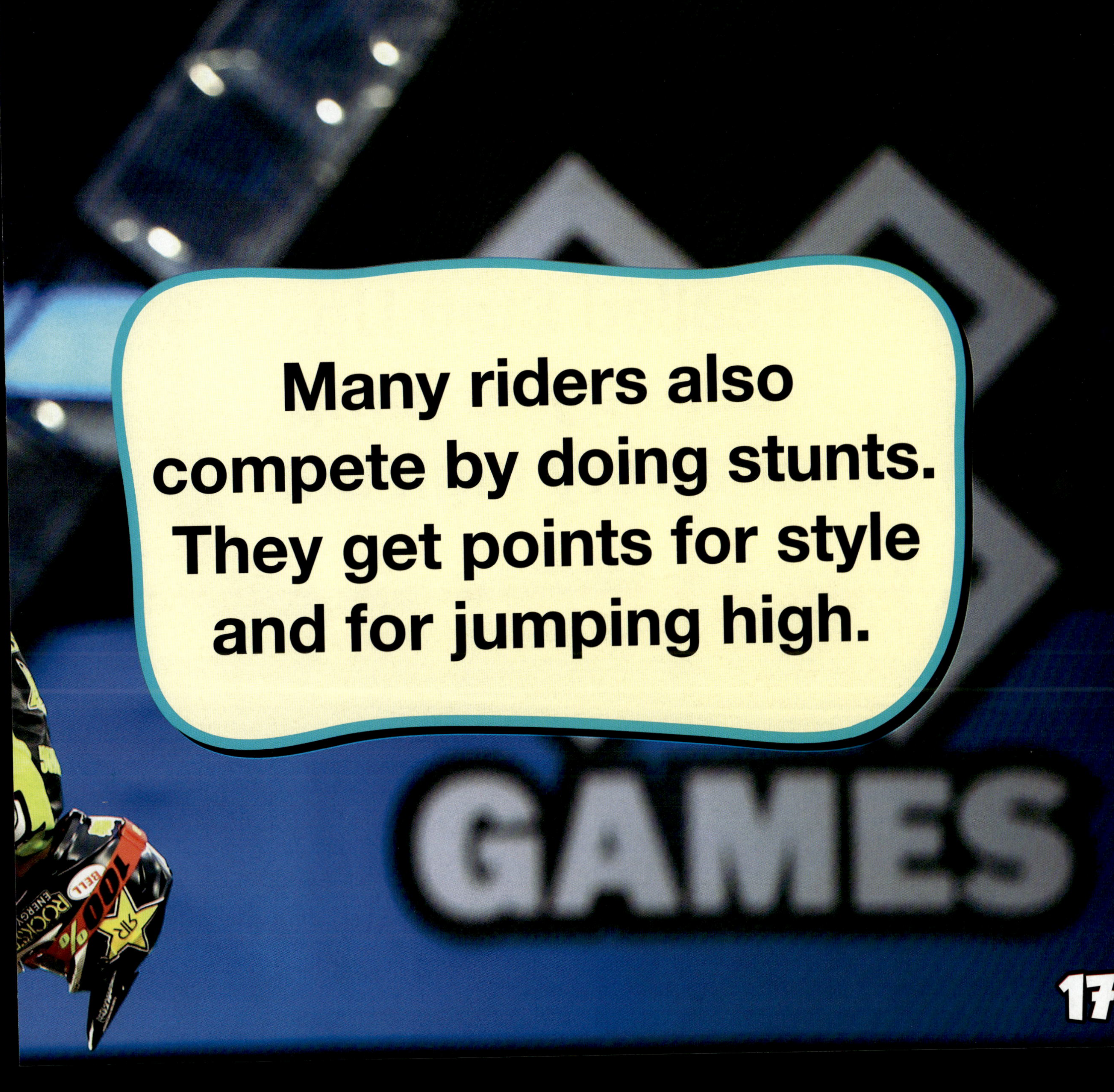

Many riders also compete by doing stunts. They get points for style and for jumping high.

Another competition is called Step Up. Riders try to jump over a very high bar.

GAMES
GAMES
UYTEN

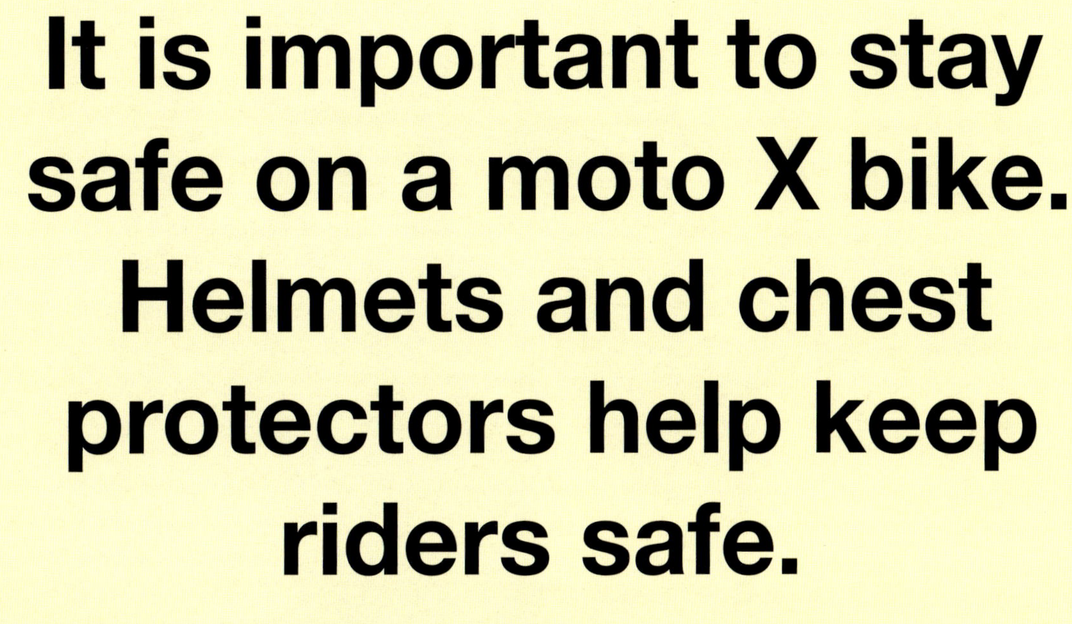

It is important to stay safe on a moto X bike. Helmets and chest protectors help keep riders safe.

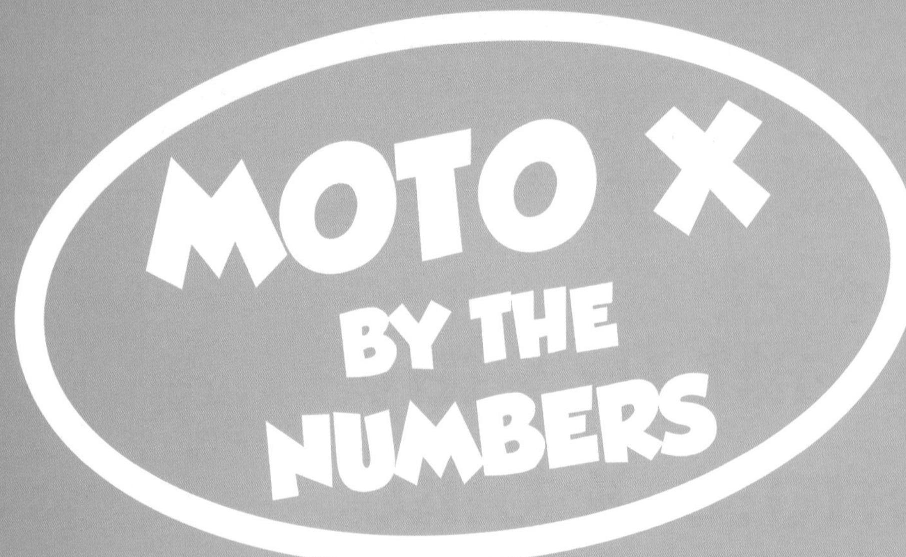

Moto X tires should be replaced after being used for 100 hours.

The first moto X races in the United States were held in 1959.

Moto X bikes weigh between 200 and 250 pounds. (90.7 and 113.4 kilograms)

Moto X bikes **do not have kickstands, speedometers, or lights.**

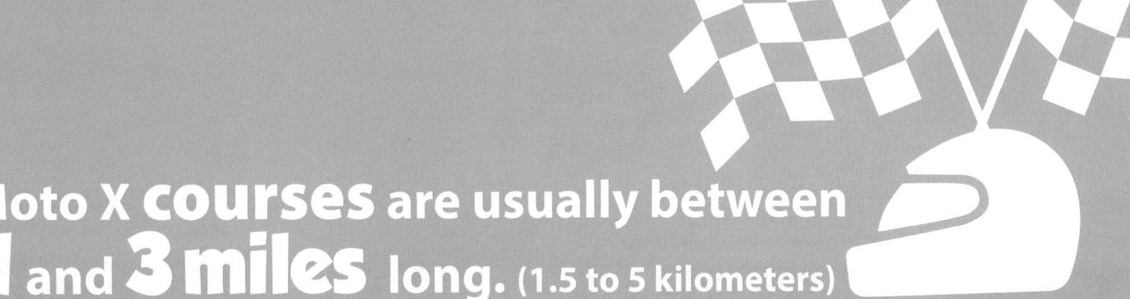

Moto X **courses** are usually between **1** and **3 miles** long. (1.5 to 5 kilometers)

People are **not allowed** to drive **moto X bikes** on **streets** or **highways.**

KEY WORDS

Research has shown that as much as 65 percent of all written material published in English is made up of 300 words. These 300 words cannot be taught using pictures or learned by sounding them out. They must be recognized by sight. This book contains 43 common sight words to help young readers improve their reading fluency and comprehension. This book also teaches young readers several important content words, such as proper nouns. These words are paired with pictures to aid in learning and improve understanding.

Page	Sight Words First Appearance
5	an, and, is, on, to, use
6	are, small, they
9	do, helps, more, much, not, these, this, very
10	others, own, make, some, their
13	day, different, every, in, them
14	each, have, many
17	also, by, for, get, high, points
18	a, another, over, try
21	important, it, keep

Page	Content Words First Appearance
5	extreme sport, moto X, motorcycles, offroad tracks, riders
6	bikes
10	indoors, outside, ramps
13	events, professional
14	courses, hills
17	stunts, style
18	bar, competition, Step Up
21	chest protectors, helmets

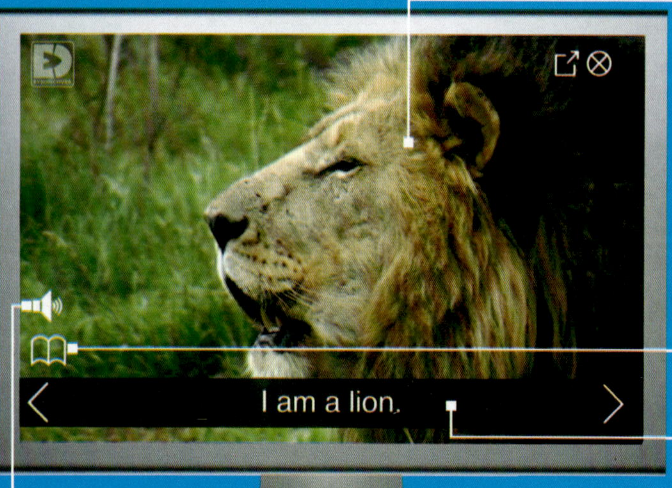

Watch
Video content brings each page to life.

Browse
Thumbnails make navigation simple.

Read
Follow along with text on the screen.

Listen
Hear each page read aloud.

Go to www.eyediscover.com and enter this book's unique code.

BOOK CODE

AVA96966